STEVEN UNIVERSE™

A CARTOON NETWORK ORIGINAL

WARP TOUR

WWW.BOOM-STUDIOS.COM

STEVEN UNIVERSE **Volume One: WARP TOUR, October 2017.** Published by KaBOOM!, a division of Boom Entertainment, Inc. STEVEN UNIVERSE, CARTOON NETWORK, the logos, and all related characters and elements are trademarks of and © Cartoon Network. (S17) Originally published in single magazine form as STEVEN UNIVERSE ONGOING No. 1-4 © Cartoon Network. (S17) All rights reserved. KaBOOM!™ and the KaBOOM! logo are trademarks of Boom Entertainment, Inc., registered in various countries and categories. All characters, events, and institutions depicted herein are fictional. Any similarity between any of the names, characters, persons, events, and/or institutions in this publication to actual names, characters, and persons, whether living or dead, events, and/or institutions is unintended and purely coincidental. KaBOOM! does not read or accept unsolicited submissions of ideas, stories, or artwork.

BOOM! Studios, 5670 Wilshire Boulevard, Suite 450, Los Angeles, CA 90036-5679. Printed in China. First Printing.

ISBN: 978-1-68415-033-5, eISBN: 978-1-61398-710-0

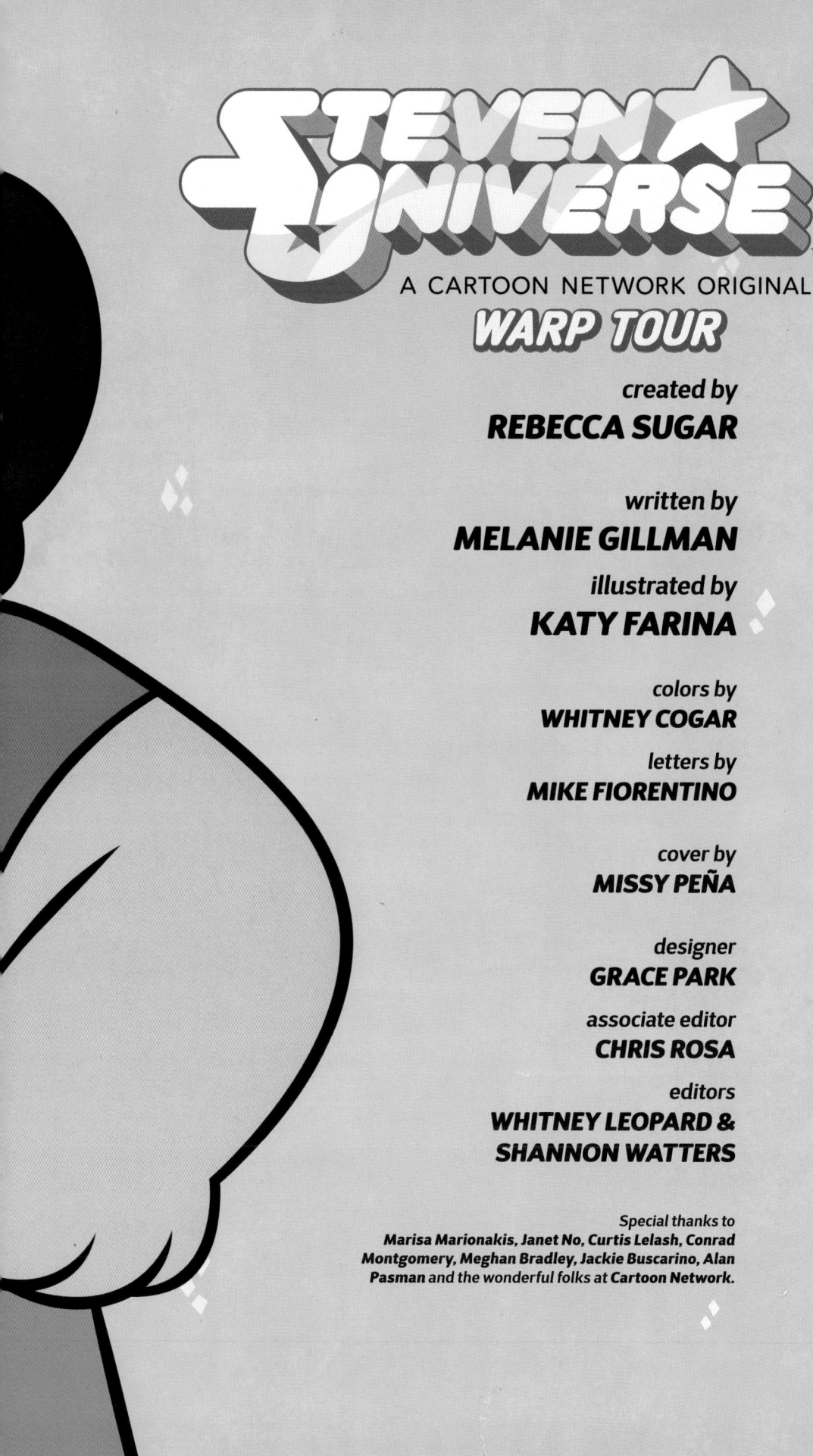

STEVEN UNIVERSE™

A CARTOON NETWORK ORIGINAL
WARP TOUR

created by
REBECCA SUGAR

written by
MELANIE GILLMAN

illustrated by
KATY FARINA

colors by
WHITNEY COGAR

letters by
MIKE FIORENTINO

cover by
MISSY PEÑA

designer
GRACE PARK

associate editor
CHRIS ROSA

editors
**WHITNEY LEOPARD &
SHANNON WATTERS**

Special thanks to
**Marisa Marionakis, Janet No, Curtis Lelash, Conrad
Montgomery, Meghan Bradley, Jackie Buscarino, Alan
Pasman** and the wonderful folks at **Cartoon Network.**

CHAPTER ONE

EMPIRE CITY WILDLIFE REHABILITATION CENTER.

UHH... STEVEN UNIVERSE! CAN WE BRING YOU A BABY BIRD WE FOUND OUTSIDE OUR BARN?

THAT DEPENDS. CAN YOU TELL WHAT SPECIES IT IS?

IT'S, UMM— A BIRD? A VERY TINY AND NAKED ONE?

IT'S *DEFECATING ON MEEEEEEEE*

WELL, YOU CAN BRING IT BY IF YOU'D LIKE, BUT I'LL BE HONEST—IF IT'S ANY SORT OF COMMON LOCAL SONGBIRD SPECIES, WE PROBABLY CAN'T TAKE IT IN.

WE GET TEN CALLS A DAY ABOUT BABY SONGBIRDS, AND FRANKLY, WE'VE GOT TO SAVE OUR RESOURCES FOR THE ANIMALS THAT ARE *ACTUALLY* ENDANGERED.

WHAT SHOULD WE DO, THEN?

WELL—IF YOU CAN'T FIND ITS NEST, THEN YOU CAN LINE A LITTLE STRAWBERRY BASKET WITH PAPER TOWELS AND LEAVE THE BABY UP IN A TREE NEAR WHERE YOU FOUND IT.

THE MOM'LL FIND IT, MAYB--UHH, PROBABLY.

MAYBE... *WE* COULD BE ITS MOM?

ABSOLUTELY NOT.

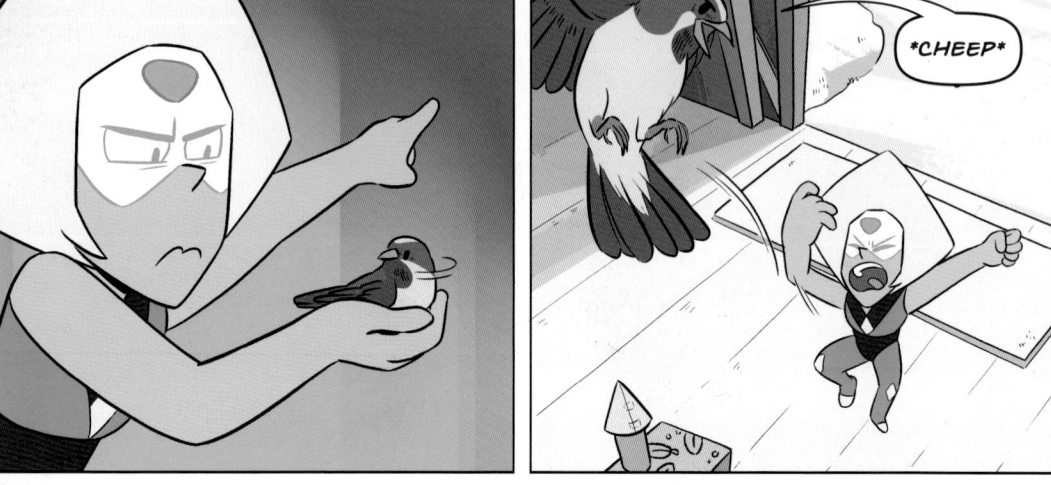

CHEEP

CHEEP

SUSAN!

STEVEN, LOOK...

CHEEP

I THINK IT'S TIME.

B-BUT... THEY'VE NEVER BEEN ON THEIR OWN BEFORE!

HOW WILL THEY TAKE CARE OF THEMSELF, WITHOUT FREE WORMS AND CABLE TV?

IT'S OKAY—THEY KNOW WHERE TO FIND US, IF THEY NEED ANYTHING.

YEAH— I GUESS SO.

SUSAN ♡

LAPIS? THE GARDEN'S OVER—

SHHHH.

LAPIS...?

C'MERE— AND HOLD OUT YOUR HAND.

UHH....

NOW HOLD VERY STILL.

GASP

THE END

CHAPTER TWO

AAAH, STEVEN, I'M SO EXCITED!

I'VE BEEN DYING TO SEE THIS EVER SINCE RUMORS ABOUT IT FIRST SURFACED DEEP ON THE *SPIRIT MORPH SAGA* FAN WIKI!

THOUGH I *AM* A LITTLE CONCERNED HOW BELIEVABLE A COMPUTER-ANIMATED ARCHIMICARUS WILL BE...

TWO FOR "THE UNFAMILIAR FAMILIAR", PLEASE!

RISING CRASHING 11:00 1:

UNFAMIC FAMILIAR PG-13 :45 3:00 6:15

SORRY, GUYS--IT'S PG-13. I CAN'T LET YOU IN WITHOUT AN ADULT.

WHAT!

UNFAMILIAR FAMILIAR

OH NO.

HOW **COULD** THEY!! THIS IS A **COMPLETE** DEPARTURE FROM THE PLATONIC WITCH-FAMILIAR RELATIONSHIP DEPICTED IN THE BOOK!

I DIDN'T REALIZE FALCONS HAD SO MANY ...ABS?

UGH, THEY ALWAYS DO THIS! PUSHING ROMANCES INTO KIDS' SERIES RIGHT AWAY--

THEY COULD'VE AT **LEAST** HAD THE DECENCY TO WAIT UNTIL THEY ACTUALLY GET TOGETHER IN **DESTINY'S END.**

TERRY SHIN IN: THE GOOD BOY

STILL--I KINDA WISH WE COULD SEE IT ANYWAY. JUST SO I KNOW HOW BAD IT REALLY IS!

WELLLLLLLLL...

THERE IS ONE WAY WE COULD STILL GET IN!

EXCUSE ME...

HELLO-- UH--FELLOW TEEN!

TW--**ONE** TICKET FOR "THE UNFAMILIAR FAMILIAR", PLEASE.

O...KAY. I JUST NEED TO SEE YOUR ID, THEN.

...MY ID?

I MEAN--HAHA-- OF COURSE! LET ME JUST--REMEMBER WHERE I PUT IT--

HMM.

BEACH CITY MIDDLE SCHOOL

"INVALID ID", PFFFT.

I GUESS IT'LL JUST HAVE TO WAIT UNTIL ONE OF US IS OLD ENOUGH FOR A DRIVER'S LICENSE.

WAIT... HOW OLD *AM* I, ANYWAY?

OOF!

UH-- YOU OKAY THERE?

CAN *I* GO SHOPPING THERE WITH YOU?

SURE, IF YOU WANT TO!

YOU SEEM WAY TOO EXCITED ABOUT THIS...

HEY-- THANKS. THAT WAS ACTUALLY PRETTY FUN!

YEAH! I'M GLAD YOU--HAHA--RAN INTO ME.

HEY--I DON'T KNOW IF YOU'RE BUSY LATER, BUT--

THE SCHOOL DANCE IS AT 7, AND I'M GONNA MEET SOME FRIENDS THERE.

YOU SHOULD COME TOO! YOU CAN SHOW OFF YOUR NEW OUTFIT.

OMIGOSH, YES! I'VE NEVER BEEN TO A SCHOOL DANCE BEFORE!

YAY! SEE YOU AT 7, THEN!

IT'S A DATE!

...SEE YOU.

OKAY, SO—

I'VE COMPILED A LIST OF EVERYTHING WE'LL NEED TO BLEND IN AT THE PROM TONIGHT, BASED ON CLASSIC TEEN MOVIES LIKE *PASTY IN PINK* AND *PIT ORCHESTRA 2: ELECTRIC BOOGALOO.*

LIMO, CORSAGE, BIG FANCY HAIR, BIG FANCY DINNER, TENOR BASSOON--

HMM, MAYBE MAKE THAT TWO...

WE'LL NEED A CHAPERONE, TOO, 'CUZ I'M NOT SUPPOSED TO BE OUT ALONE AFTER DARK.

NO PROBLEM.

PEARL! I HAVE AN IMPORTANT MISSION FOR YOU AND YOUR TUX!

C'MON--I'LL INTRODUCE YOU TO MY FRIENDS!

GO HAVE FUN! I'LL BE RIGHT HERE IF YOU NEED ME.

THEY GROW UP SO FAST, DON'T THEY?

DO YOU, UMM--LIKE TO DANCE LEAD OR FOLLOW?

I'M NOT REALLY SURE HOW TO DO EITHER!

HAHA-- WE CAN DO THIS, THEN.

I HAD A LOT OF FUN TODAY.

YEAH! I'M, UH, GLAD YOU RAN INTO--

WAIT, AUGH-- I ALREADY MADE THAT JOKE--

HAHAHA!

IT'D BE REALLY COOL IF WE COULD DO THIS AGAIN SOMETIME?

NOT *DANCING*, I MEAN, BUT--Y'KNOW-- HANGING OUT?

I--UHH--

I'VE GOTTA GO CHECK ON PEARL REALLY QUICK, SORRY!

OH NO OH NO OH NO, WHAT ARE WE GONNA *DO?*

SHOULD WE HAVE TOLD HER RIGHT FROM THE BEGINNING??

DO WE HAVE TO START TELLING *EVERYONE* RIGHT FROM THE BEGINNING?!

WE CAN'T TELL HER! SHE'D--

WHAT IF SHE JUST-- THOUGHT WE LIED TO HER?

WHAT IF SHE HATED US?

B-BUT... WE *DIDN'T* LIE. WE JUST DIDN'T TELL HER--

AND WHAT WERE WE SUPPOSED TO SAY, ANYWAY?

"HI, MY NAME'S STEVONNIE, I'M ACTUALLY TWO KIDS FUSED INTO A TEEN VIA ALIEN MAGIC, HOW ARE YOU"?!?!

WAIT--I'VE GOT IT! WE'LL JUST KEEP GOING ON DATES WITH HER FOREVER, AND WE'LL *NEVER* TELL HER, SO THEN SHE'LL NEVER--

NO, YOU'RE RIGHT, THAT'S A TERRIBLE IDEA TOO.

WE HAVE TO TELL HER *SOMETHING*--BUT ANYTHING WE SAY MIGHT HURT HER FEELINGS OR MAKE HER MAD...

MAYBE...

MAYBE-- ALL WE'VE BEEN DOING HERE IS TRYING TO GUESS WHAT KIKI'D WANT US TO DO?

MAYBE, INSTEAD, WE SHOULD TALK ABOUT WHAT *WE* WANT TO DO?

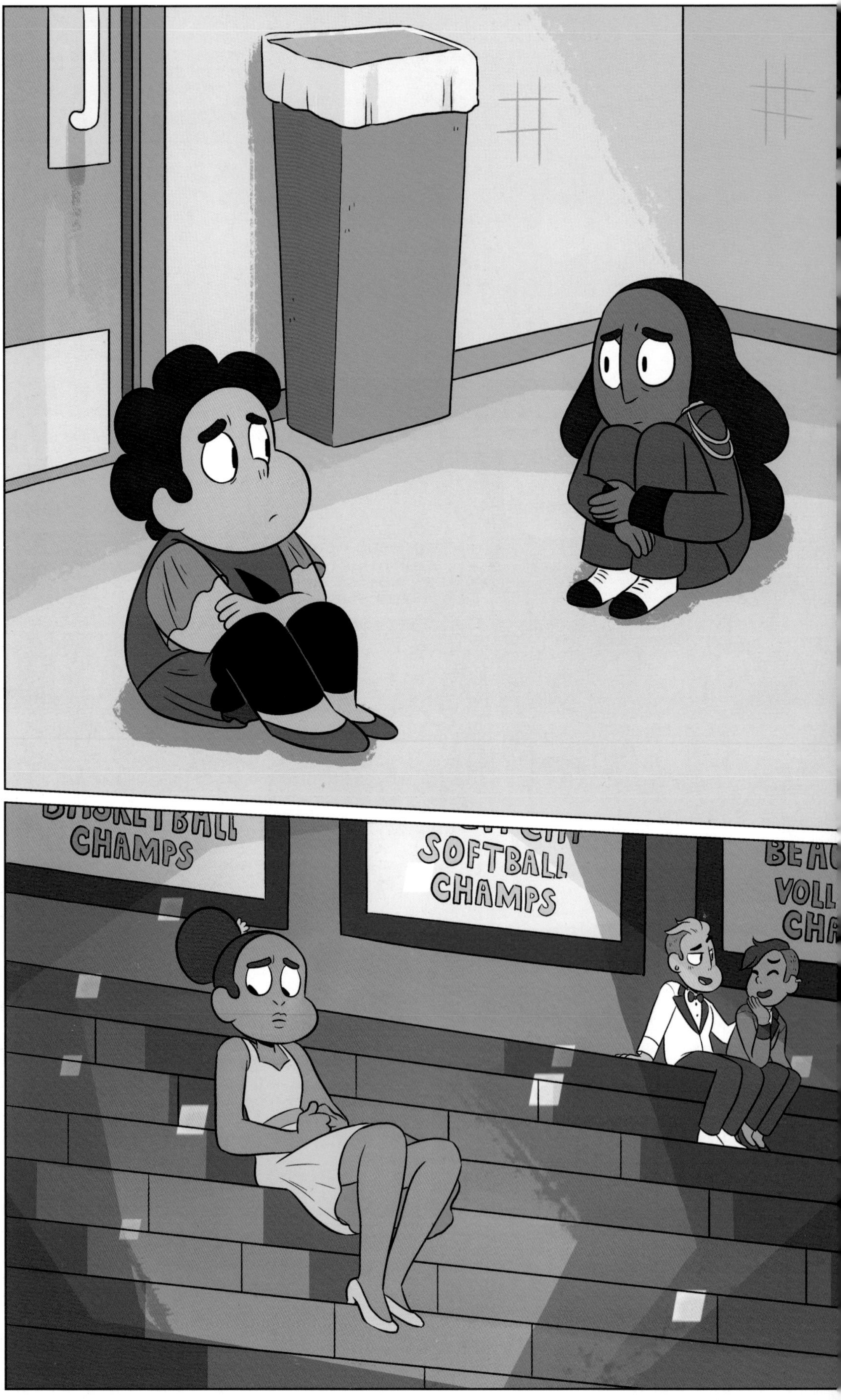
CHAMPS
SOFTBALL
CHAMPS

KIKI?

STEVONNIE! I'M REALLY SORRY, I DIDN'T MEAN TO--

IT'S OKAY! KIKI--

KIKI, I THINK YOU'RE REALLY COOL AND PRETTY AND FUN AND I'D TOTALLY LOVE TO KEEP HANGING OUT WITH YOU OR GOING DANCING OR TRYING ON EATING DONUTS OR ANYTHING, REALLY--

--AS YOUR FRIEND.

...OH.

CHAPTER THREE

HOW ARE THINGS HERE, NANEFUA? SELLING PLENTY OF MAYOR DEWEY SPECIALS TO OTHER CUSTOMERS, TOO?

EH, IT IS THE OFF-SEASON. IN SPRING IT WILL PICK UP.

THE TOURISTS, YOU KNOW—THERE IS NOT MUCH TO BRING THEM HERE WHEN IT IS COLD.

(THEM, OR THEIR WALLETS)

BEACHES ARE THE ONLY THING THIS TOWN HAS GOING FOR IT.

WHOA, NOW, SON! LET'S NOT BE A NEGATIVE NELLY!

WHY, BEACH CITY IS A CULTURAL AND HISTORIC LANDMARK!

WE HAVE A THRIVING BOARDWALK FULL OF SHOPS AND RESTAURANTS!

MILES OF COASTLINE AND PRISTINE OCEAN VIEWS!

WE HAVE— UH—

...WE HAVE A MUSEUM OF EXTRATERRESTRIAL SCIENCE AND TECHNOLOGY?

I THINK RONALDO RUNS THAT!

THE POINT IS, I SAY BEACH CITY HAS A LITTLE SOMETHING FOR EVERYONE— YEAR-ROUND!

YOU'D THINK THEY'D BE HERE, THEN.

AH— WELL—

WELL, I ALWAYS VALUE THE INPUT OF OUR LOCAL YOUTH!

TELL ME— WHAT WOULD *YOU* DO TO MAKE THIS GREAT CITY OF OURS MORE OF A "COOL" PLACE TO VISIT AND SPEND MONEY IN THE OFF-SEASON?

YOU KNOW, LIKE A SOCK-HOP, OR A TOWN PICNIC—

REPTILE PETTING Z—

FOOD TRUCKS.

RESTAURANTS ARE A THING OF THE PAST. MOBILE CUISINE IS THE FUTURE.

NO RULES, NO REGULATIONS- JUST THE OPEN ROAD, AND LOTS OF CILANTRO.

MAKE THAT HAPPEN, AND YOU'LL GET YOUR CROWDS, ANY TIME OF THE YEAR.

OKAY, BUT I DON'T SEE HOW WELL THAT WILL BRING PEOPLE IN *HERE*.

WELL- IT'S-

IT'S CERTAINLY WORTH A TRY!

AFTER ALL, WHO COULD VISIT BEACH CITY AND NOT FALL IN LOVE? JUST LIKE I FELL IN LOVE-

-WITH ALL MY VOTERS.

AWWWWW

BEACH CITY
FOOD TRUCK RALLY
DEWEY PARK
EVERY SAT. 12pm-5pm
555-0855
555-0855
555-0855
555-0855
555-0855
555-0855
QUINOAFFLES
Menu:
70's DINNER PARTY
70's Dinner PARTY!
Haute Daugs
Haute Daugs
Decadent Sandwiches

YOU, SIR! HOW ABOUT SAMPLING SOME OF BEACH CITY'S FINEST, ROUNDEST CUISINE?

OR YOU, MA'AM! FISH STEW PIZZA: BETTER THAN IT SOUNDS™!

HOW ABOUT YOU, SIR! YOU LOOK LIKE A GENTLEMAN OF DISCERNING TASTE–

...ANYBODY?

GASP DAD! DAAAAAAAAD!

OH, HEY SCHTOO-BALL!

DIDN'T REALIZE YOU WERE GONNA BE WORKING THE COUNTER, TOO!

QUICK, DAD—CAN YOU BUY A PIZZA?

FROM FISH STEW? I DUNNO—I WAS THINKING I'D TRY ONE OF THOSE NEW PLACES...

YOU CAN DO THAT TOO! BUT THE WHOLE POINT OF THE FOOD TRUCK RALLY IS TO HELP LOCAL BUSINESSES—

—AND IF NO ONE BUYS ANY PIZZA THEN FISH STEW WON'T MAKE ANY MONEY AND NANEFUA WILL BE SAD AND I'LL BE A BAD VOLUNTEER-EMPLOYEE AND MAYBE I'LL EVEN GET VOLUN-FIRED???

WHOA WHOA WHOA! OKAY, THEN—

IF IT'LL HELP OUT OUR NEIGHBORS, THEN SURE—GIMME A PEPPERONI PIZZA.

ONE PEPPERONI PIZZA, COMING RIGHT UP!

LET ME JUST, UH...RUN INTO THE BACK TO GET IT.

ONE PEPPERONI PIZZA, FRESH OUTTA THE OVEN!

BUCK, MY BOY! WHAT A FANTASTIC IDEA THIS WAS!

WE MADE SO MUCH MONEY, AND WE BROUGHT ALL THESE FRESH NEW FACES INTO BEACH CITY, AND WE MADE SO MUCH *MONEY...*

DAD, QUIT IT–

AH, NANEFUA! HOW ABOUT MY SON'S GREAT IDEA TO TURN OUR OFF-SEASON BACK "ON" AGAIN?

ACTUALLY, WE ONLY SOLD ONE PIZZA ALL DAY.

SORRY...

SAME HERE. I SAW PLENTY OF PEOPLE EATING FRIES, BUT WHEREVER THEY BOUGHT 'EM, IT SURE WASN'T FROM US.

EVEN OUR USUAL HALF-PRICE-AFTER-3PM CROWD NEVER SHOWED UP.

I MEAN, *I'M* NOT COMPLAINING...

UH...WELL... THIS IS...

THIS IS ONLY THE BEGINNING. NEXT TIME, WE'LL MAKE AN EVEN BIGGER STATEMENT.

SOMETHING THAT'LL REALLY PUT THIS CITY ON THE MAP.

...LIKE FOOD *AIRPLANES.*

AIRPLANES?? WHEN APPARENTLY WE CAN'T EVEN COMPETE WITH SOME LOUSY TR–

I THINK WHAT MY SON IS TRYING TO SAY IS THAT– UH–

WE'LL REINVEST! MORE ADVERTISING WILL BRING MORE CUSTOMERS NEXT TIME, AND MORE CUSTOMERS WILL BRING, UH... MORE MONEY!

MONEY FOR THE *WHOLE CITY*, NEXT TIME...!

THE NEXT MORNING.

BEACH CITY
FOOD TRUCK RALLY

DEWEY PARK
EVERY SAT. 12pm-5pm

BIG DONUT

EAT A BIG DONUT

HEY SADIE! COULD I INTEREST YOU IN A TRADE?

PERHAPS... ONE OF MY ZINES AND ALSO SOME MONEY FOR A DONUT?

HAHA, IT'S EVEN GOT BIRD PUNS!

WELL, I'D SAY THIS IS WORTH AT LEAST *TWO* DONUTS.

NO NEED, CITIZENS!

BEACH CITY OFF-SEASON COMMUNITY PICNIC!

TODAY! DEWEY PARK

TODAY, *I'M* BUYING.

OH, WHOA! IT'S PACKED!

THIS PLACE MUST BE *THE BITS*.

HEY, DO YOU KNOW HOW LONG THE WAIT IS FOR A TABLE?

UHH—LOOK, YOU REALLY DON'T WANT TO COME IN HERE. THIS IS JUST, LIKE, THIS BORING TOWN PICNIC THING THE MAYOR THREW TOGETHER—

...A PICNIC?

THE END

CHAPTER FOUR

PICK OUT ANYTHING YOU LIKE!

Designs for thy face

gns for thy face

WHAT!!

Face Paint

AWW, PERIDOT, YOU'RE SO CUT—

NOT THAT WORD.

STUPID FESTIVAL— STUPID CLODDY HISTORY—

FINALLY! SOMETHING *USEFUL!*

Lady Hachette's Weaponry

Wood S...

OOOOOOOOH!

NYEH HEH HEH HEH

SIR! RENDER!!!!!

BOOOOOOOOOOOOOOOOOOO

AND HERE TO FACE THEM—BEACH CITADEL'S OWN *LADY!* HACHETTE!!!!!

YAAAAAAAAAAAAAAYy

ON YOUR MARKS...

GET SET...

JOUST!

BOOOOOOOO

BOOOOOOOO

YEAH!!!

THE SCORE SO FAR IS... SIR RENDER: SEVEN, EVERYONE ELSE: ZERO.

BOOOOOOOO

ALAS! IF NO ONE ELSE DARES CHALLENGE THEM, I FEAR OUR FAIR BEACH CITADEL WILL NEVER HAVE ITS OWN CHAMPION!

IS THERE ANYONE LEFT OF STOUT ENOUGH HEART TO TAKE THE FIELD??

GASP

COULD IT BE?? SIR SHALLOT OF CASTLE VIDALIA!

OH NO...CAN'T THEY GIVE THE PONY A HELMET TOO?

CRUSH THE UPSTART UNDER YOUR MIGHTY HEEL!!

OKAY, KIDS—WHO ELSE WANTS TO TRY BEING A BRAVE KNIGHT TODAY?

ME!! ME!! I'M NEXT!!

ANOTHER NEW CHALLENGER HAS APPEARED TO TEST THEIR METTLE ON THE FIELD OF HONOR!

YOUR LANCE, M'LADY.

THANK YOU, SQUIRE.

IS THIS PRIMITIVE ASSAULT STICK SUPPOSED TO BE SO HEAVY??

ON YOUR MARKS—GET SET—

JOUST!

EEP!

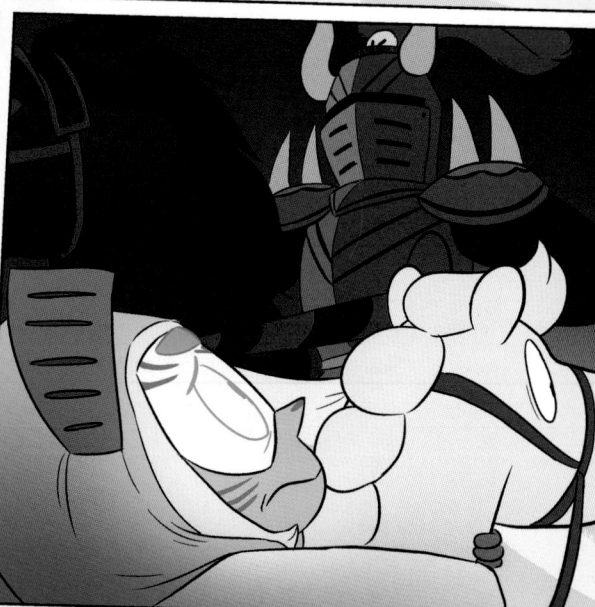

THAT WAS AWESOME!

YOU CREAMED THAT JERK!

YEAH!! TAKE *THAT*, OCEAN TOWN!!

BUT... I DIDN'T EVEN HIT THEM?

CHEATER!!!

YOU LET BEINGS SMALLER AND WEAKER THAN YOU WIN ON PURPOSE!

I DEMAND A REMATCH!!

NO, NO! YOU WON BECAUSE, UHH—YOU'RE SUCH A *BRAVE* LITTLE KNIGHT!

DON'T YOU PATRONIZE ME JUST BECAUSE I'M—UGH—CUTE.

I'LL SEE YOU ON *THE DUELING GROUND.*

FAIR BEACH CITY-ANS! WE HAVE GATHERED HERE ONE LAST TIME TODAY FOR A THRILLING, FINAL REMATCH—

—TO THE STAGE— DEATH!!

TO MY RIGHT— SIR RENDER OF THE TOWNSHIP OF OCEAN, WHO RECENTLY SUFFERED A HUMILIATING DEFEAT!

AND TO MY LEFT— SIR PERIDOT OF THE BARN, WHO BELIEVES SHE HAD HER HUMILIATING DEFEAT WRONGFULLY STOLEN FROM HER!

ONLY ONE MAY BE CROWNED THE TRUE LOSER OF THE DAY!!

ON YOUR MARK—GET SET—

JOUST!!!

Y'KNOW WHAT? NO. SORRY, THIS IS WAY TOO WEIRD FOR ME.

SORRY, GUYS— I DON'T THINK I CAN LET YOU BACK IN FOR A WHILE, AT LEAST UNTIL SIR RENDER'S NOSE HEALS.

NO—I'M SORRY.

I SEE NOW I LET MY TEMPER GET THE BETTER OF ME.

I...HOPE YOU'LL FORGIVE ME FOR CAUSING TROUBLE.

(AND TRYING TO HIT YOU WITH MY SWORD.)

I'M STILL LEARNING HOW TO CONTROL MYSELF, BUT I PROMISE THIS WON'T HAPPEN AGAIN.

WOW, PERIDOT. THAT WAS... ALMOST MATURE OF YOU?

YEP, THAT'S ME.

Beach City Renaissance Faire

EVERY DAY, A BETTER, MORE MATURE GEM.

THE END

COVER GALLERY

issue one fried pie exclusive cover
MISSY PEÑA

issue one wondercon exclusive cover
MISSY PEÑA

issue one gem foil exclusive cover
MISSY PEÑA

issue two main cover
MISSY PEÑA

FLEXIBILITY, LOVE & TRUST

issue one subscription cover
RIAN SYGH

issue two subscription cover
RIAN SYGH

issue three subscription cover
RIAN SYGH

issue four subscription cover
RIAN SYGH

issue one variant cover
JENN ST-ONGE

issue two variant cover
JENN ST-ONGE

issue three variant cover
JENN ST-ONGE

issue four variant cover
JENN ST-ONGE

DISCOVER
EXPLOSIVE NEW WORLDS